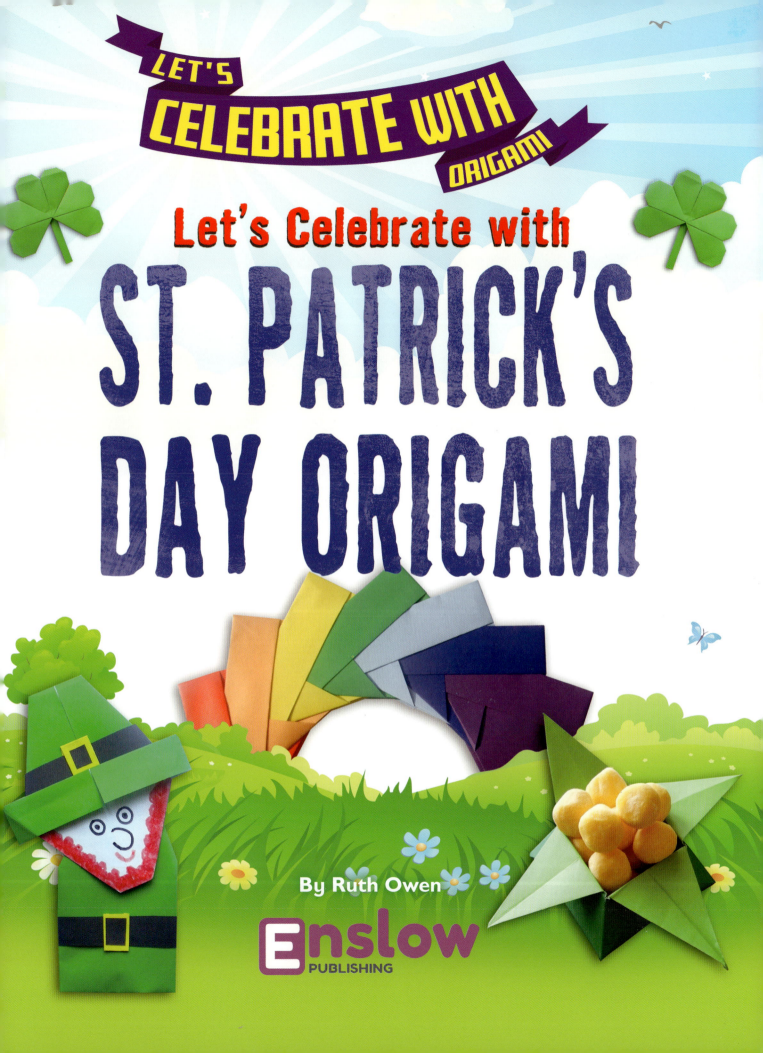

Published in 2022 by Enslow Publishing, LLC
29 East 21st Street
New York, NY 10010

Copyright © 2022 Enslow Publishing, LLC
All rights reserved.

Produced for Rosen by Ruth Owen Books
Designer: Emma Randall
Photos courtesy of Ruth Owen Books and Shutterstock

Cataloging-in-Publication Data

Names: Owen, Ruth.
Title: Let's celebrate with St. Patrick's Day origami / Ruth Owen.
Description: New York : Enslow Publishing, 2022. | Series: Let's celebrate with origami | Includes glossary and index.
Identifiers: ISBN 9781978526679 (pbk.) | ISBN 9781978526693 (library bound) | ISBN 9781978526686 (6 pack) | ISBN 9781978526709 (ebook)
Subjects: LCSH: Origami--Juvenile literature. | Saint Patrick's Day decorations--Juvenile literature.
Classification: LCC TT870.O946 2022 | DDC 736'.982--dc23

All rights reserved. No part of this book may be reproduced in any form without permission in writing from the publisher, except by a reviewer.

Manufactured in the United States of America

CPSIA compliance information: Batch #CWENS22: For further information contact Enslow Publishing, New York, New York at 1-800-398-2504

Find us on

Contents

An Origami Holiday 4

Origami Tips 6

Fold a Celtic Cross 8

Let's Make Shamrocks 12

A Paper Leprechaun 16

Make a Pot of Gold 20

A Rainbow Celebration 24

Make Green Ribbons 28

Glossary, Index, Websites 32

An Origami Holiday

St. Patrick's Day is a huge celebration in Ireland and in other parts of the world where Irish people have settled. It is a religious celebration that **commemorates** the death of St. Patrick, the patron saint of Ireland. It is held on March 17th every year.

This year, you can get ready for St. Patrick's Day by making fun decorations using **origami**, the art of folding paper. No one knows where origami got started, but it has been popular for centuries in Japan. In fact, "origami" is Japanese for "folding paper."

If you've never tried origami before, don't be nervous. Just follow the step-by-step instructions and you'll soon be folding St. Patrick's Day paper shamrocks and leprechauns!

Origami Tips

Check out these tips that will help you make your St. Patrick's Day models.

Tip 1
Read all the instructions carefully and look at the pictures. Make sure you understand what's required before you begin a fold. Don't rush; be patient. Work slowly and carefully.

Tip 2
Folding a piece of paper sounds easy, but it can be tricky to get neat, accurate folds. The more you practice, the easier it becomes.

Tip 3
If an instruction says "crease," make the crease as flat as possible. The flatter the creases, the better the model. You can make a sharp crease by running a plastic ruler along the edge of the paper.

Tip 4
Sometimes, at first, your models may look a little crumpled. Don't give up! The more models you make, the better you will get at folding and creasing.

When it comes to origami, practice makes perfect!

Some people become so expert at folding paper, they can make complicated models like the pineapple, colorful ball, and swans shown here. But whatever your level of expertise, origami is a popular hobby that people of all ages can enjoy.

All these models were made just by folding paper. Keep practicing and you could soon become an origami master.

Some origami models are made from hundreds of small sections, or modules.

7

Fold a Celtic Cross

This first project shows you how to make a mini origami paper cross. The **Celtic** cross is one of the **symbols** that is often associated with St. Patrick's Day. Why?

St. Patrick was born in Britain during the 4th century. He became a priest and traveled to Ireland. Here, he spread the Christian religion and converted many Irish people to Christianity. Before St. Patrick came to Ireland, many people there believed in **pagan** religions. They celebrated nature and worshipped the sun.

Legends say that St. Patrick combined the Christian cross with the sun to create a religious symbol that celebrated both nature and God the creator.

To make a Celtic cross, you will need:

One sheet of origami paper in your choice of color

Scissors

Glue

(Origami paper is sometimes colored on both sides or white on one side.)

STEP 1:

Cut the sheet of paper in half and work with one half. This paper is green on one side and yellow on the other. We want to make a green cross, so we placed the paper green side down.

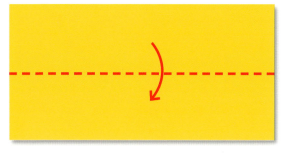

Fold the paper in half, crease well, and unfold.

STEP 2:

Now fold the top and the bottom halves of the paper into the center, and crease.

STEP 3:

Fold the right-hand side of the model over to the left along the dotted line, and crease hard. Then fold the right-hand side back again, making a small pleat.

pleat

STEP 4:

Fold in the two points in the center of the model, and crease hard.

9

STEP 5:
Fold the bottom right-hand edge of the model up and into the center. As you do this, the folded point should open out. As it does, squash it flat to form a triangle.

Repeat on the top right-hand side of the model.

STEP 6:
Now fold the left-hand side of the model over to the right along the dotted line, and crease. Then fold the left-hand side back again, making a small pleat.

STEP 7:
Fold in the two points in the center of the model, and crease hard.

Then repeat what you did in step 5 on the left-hand side of your model.

Turn your model over, and it will look like this.

10

STEP 8:
To make the sunlike center section of the cross, take the other half of the piece of paper and cut it in half so you now have a quarter-sized square piece. Fold the paper into four quarters. Then fold each corner into the center of the model, creasing hard.

STEP 9:
Turn the model over and fold the four corners into the center again, creasing hard.

STEP 10:
Turn the model over again, and fold the four corners into the center, creasing hard.

STEP 11:
Finally, turn the model over one more time. Fold each corner behind to create a rounded shape. Then glue the sun to the center of the cross.

Fold the top of the cross behind to make it shorter.

Let's Make Shamrocks

Why is a three-leaf shamrock a symbol of the St. Patrick's Day holiday? Legend says that St. Patrick used the leaves of this tiny green plant to explain the holy trinity to the Irish people. He used the shamrock as a symbol of the Father, the Son, and the Holy Spirit.

A three-leaf shamrock is now the symbol of Ireland. It has also become a favorite St. Patrick's Day decoration.

To make an origami shamrock, you will need:

Four sheets of green paper with pale green on the reverse side

Glue or tape

12

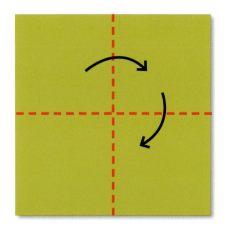

STEP 1:

The shamrock is made from three modules, or sections. To make one module, place the paper green side down. Fold the paper in half from side to side, crease, and unfold. Then fold in half from top to bottom, crease, and unfold.

STEP 2:

Fold down the top half of the paper so it meets the center, and crease. Then turn the paper over.

STEP 3:

Now fold down the two top corners into the center of the model, and crease well.

STEP 4:

Turn the model over, and it should look like this.

Now fold down the top of the model so it meets the bottom, and crease well.

13

STEP 5:
Turn the model over again. Now lift up the small rectangular flap on the left-hand side. As you lift up the flap, you will see a small triangle forming. Gently flatten this triangle.

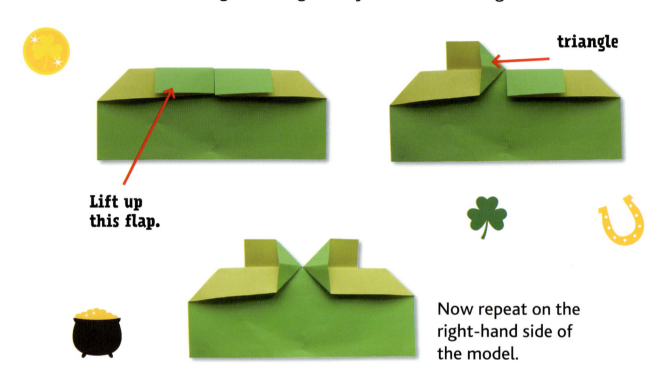

Lift up this flap.

triangle

Now repeat on the right-hand side of the model.

STEP 6:
Fold in the sides of the model along the dotted lines, and crease hard.

STEP 7:
Fold in the two top corners of the model along the dotted lines, and crease.

STEP 8:
Now fold down the two top points of the model, and crease.

STEP 9:
Turn the model over and your first module is complete. Now repeat steps 1 to 8 two more times so you have three heart-shaped modules in total.

STEP 10:
To join the modules together, slide the pale green triangle of one module under the dark green heart of another. Glue or tape the modules together.

STEP 11:
When all three modules are joined, fold the remaining two bottom triangles behind the model.

STEP 12:
Finally, fold or roll up a small piece of green paper to make a stalk, and tape or glue it behind the shamrock leaves.

15

A Paper Leprechaun

Irish legends include many tales of leprechauns and other fairy folk. Leprechauns are said to look like tiny men who wear green suits and have orange or red beards. They collect money and gold, and then they hide it away.

When St. Patrick's Day comes around, you might see people wearing big green hats and green suits. That's because they are dressing up as leprechauns!

This next project shows you how to make a paper leprechaun using origami and some cutting and gluing.

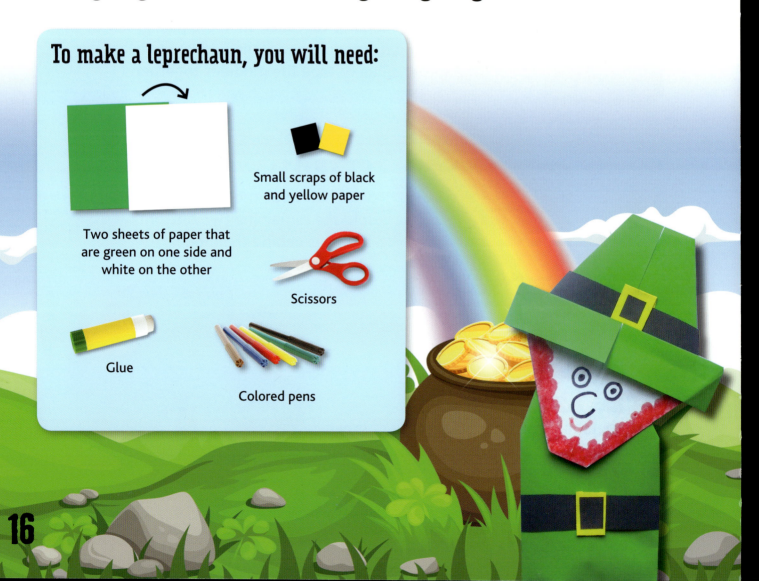

To make a leprechaun, you will need:

- Two sheets of paper that are green on one side and white on the other
- Small scraps of black and yellow paper
- Scissors
- Glue
- Colored pens

16

STEP 1:
To make the leprechaun's head, place the paper green side down. Fold the paper in half diagonally, crease, and unfold.

STEP 2:
Now fold in the two sides of the model so they meet in the center, and crease well.

STEP 3:
Fold up the bottom half of the model along the dotted line, and crease.

STEP 4:
Now fold the top layer of paper back down along the dotted line, and crease.

Your model should now look like this.

17

STEP 5:
Turn the model over. Fold in the sides of the model along the dotted lines, and crease well.

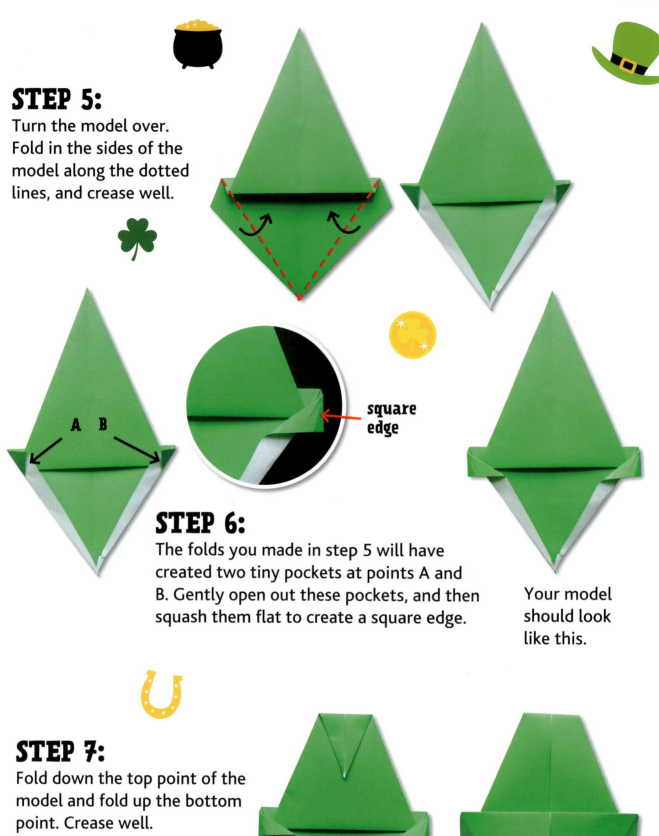

STEP 6:
The folds you made in step 5 will have created two tiny pockets at points A and B. Gently open out these pockets, and then squash them flat to create a square edge.

Your model should look like this.

STEP 7:
Fold down the top point of the model and fold up the bottom point. Crease well.

Turn the model over, and the leprechaun's head is complete.

STEP 8:
To make the leprechaun's body, repeat steps 1 and 2 with the second piece of paper. Then fold up the bottom of the model, and crease.

STEP 9:
Now fold down the top point of the model so it overlaps the bottom point, and crease well.

STEP 10:
Fold in the sides of the model along the dotted lines, and crease. The sides will now allow your leprechaun model to stand up.

STEP 11:
Now slide the body into the back of the head. You can use a little glue or tape to hold it in place.

STEP 12:
Turn the model over. To decorate the leprechaun, draw on a face and beard. Glue on small pieces of black and yellow paper to decorate the hat and make a belt.

Make a Pot of Gold

In this next project you can make a cute little pot, or box, to fill with gold candy. But why are pots of gold a part of our St. Patrick's Day celebrations?

Old Irish legends say that if you capture a leprechaun and keep your eye on him, the little creature won't be able to vanish. In order to win his freedom, the leprechaun will tell you where his pot of gold is hidden.

To make a pot of gold, you will need:

One sheet of paper in your choice of color

Small pieces of yellow candy or cereal

STEP 1:

Begin by placing the paper with the color of your pot facing up. We chose to make a dark green pot with pale green inside. Fold the paper diagonally from side to side, crease, and unfold. Then fold from top to bottom, crease, and unfold.

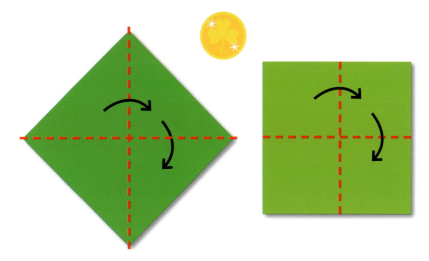

Turn the paper over. Fold the paper from side to side, crease, and unfold. Then fold from top to bottom, crease, and unfold.

STEP 2:

Now fold and close up the paper by bringing points A and B to meet each other, and point C down to meet point D.

Your flattened model should now look like this.

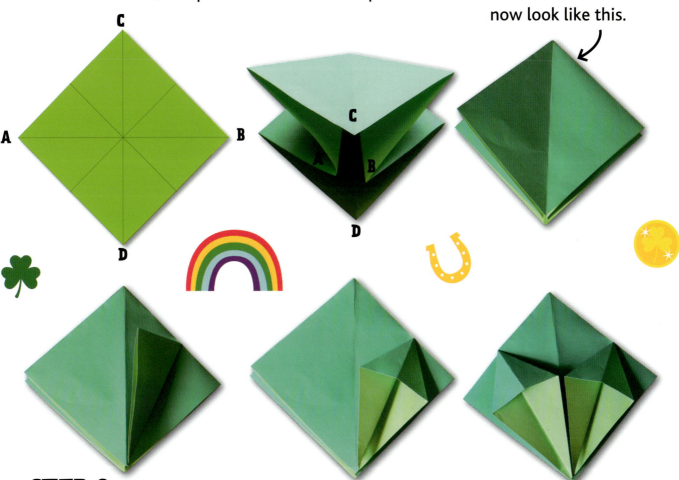

STEP 3:

Working with the top layer of paper only, fold the right-hand side of the model into the center, and crease well.

Then open out the fold you've just made, and squash it flat to create a kite shape.

Repeat on the left-hand side of the model.

21

STEP 4:

Turn the model over and repeat step 3 on the other side. Your model should now look like this.

STEP 5:

Now, pick up your model, and you will see that it has four sides, or faces. Two will have kite shapes, and two will be flat. Adjust the model so that there is a flat face on top and on the bottom, and lay the model down again. Your model should look like this.

Now, working only with the top layer of paper, fold the right-hand side of the model into the center, and crease.

Repeat on the left-hand side.

Turn the model over and fold the sides into the center, creasing well.

22

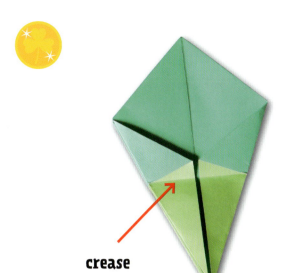

STEP 6:
Now fold up the bottom point of the model so it meets the top point, crease hard, and unfold.

crease

STEP 7:
Now take hold of the bottom points of the model and gently pull them apart. You will see that the top half of the model is forming the box shape.

This next part is tricky, but slide your fingers inside the model and carefully press out and shape the box until it looks like this.

Fill your box with yellow candy or cereal, and your St. Patrick's Day pot of gold is complete!

A Rainbow Celebration

Legends say that leprechauns are crafty and will do all they can to keep the hiding places of their gold a secret. They will even play tricks on humans. A leprechaun might say his gold is hidden at the end of a rainbow. But of course, no matter how hard you search, you will never find the end of a rainbow!

Complete your St. Patrick's Day leprechaun story by making this colorful origami rainbow to go with your paper leprechaun and pot of gold.

To make a rainbow, you will need:
Seven sheets of origami paper in rainbow colors (red, orange, yellow, green, blue, indigo, and violet)
Glue or tape

STEP 1:

We made a rainbow with seven sections, or modules. To make one module, place a piece of paper colored side down. Fold it in half from side to side, crease, and unfold. Then fold from top to bottom, crease, and unfold.

STEP 2:

Fold the top two corners of the paper into the center creases, and crease well.

STEP 3:

Fold up the bottom half of the model to meet the center crease, then crease and unfold.

STEP 4:

Now fold up the bottom of the model along the red dotted line, and crease.

crease made in step 3

25

STEP 5:
Turn the model over. Fold in the two small triangles on the sides of the model.

STEP 6:
Fold up the bottom of the model along the dotted line, tucking the two small triangles inside. Crease well.

STEP 7:
Now fold the model in half along the dotted line by folding the right-hand side of the model behind. This first module is now complete.

STEP 8:
Repeat steps 1 to 7 to make the remaining six modules.

26

The two ends of the module are here.

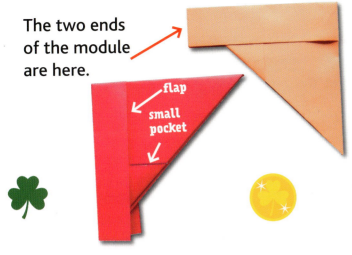

STEP 9:
To join the modules together, take two modules and position them as shown. You will see there is a flap and small pocket on the left-hand side of the red module.

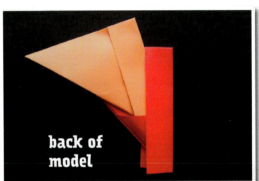

Now slide the orange module over the top of the red module so that the red module is between the two ends of the orange module. Slide one end of the orange module into the flap and pocket on the front of the red module. Slide the other end section into the flap and pocket on the back of the red module.

Keep sliding so that the orange module is snugly tucked inside the red module.

Repeat until all the sections are joined together. If you wish, you can tape or glue the modules together to help hold them in place.

Make Green Ribbons

Ireland is often called "the Emerald Isle" because of its grassy, rolling hills and green fields. In fact, people say that Ireland's landscape has 40 shades of green!

Green is an important color for Ireland. It appears on Ireland's flag and is also the country's national color. Green is also used a lot in St. Patrick's Day decorations.

In this final project, make a green St. Patrick's Day ribbon to wear during your celebrations. Have fun making your ribbon, and have a great St. Patrick's Day!

To make a ribbon, you will need:

Origami paper in different shades of green

Scissors

Glue

A piece of thin cardboard measuring about 4 inches square (10 sq cm)
• A pen   • Tape   • A safety pin

STEP 1:

To make a ribbon that measures about 4 inches (10 cm) across, you will need 12 pieces of paper each measuring 3 inches by 2 inches (7.5 cm x 5 cm).

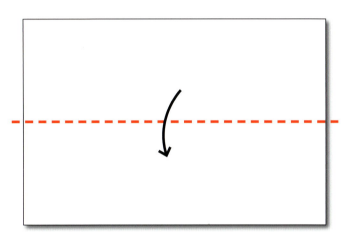

STEP 2:

To make one module of the ribbon, place a piece of paper colored side down, fold it in half along the dotted line, and crease hard. Now fold the model in half again along the dotted line, crease, and then unfold.

STEP 3:

Fold down the right-hand side of the model to meet the center crease you've just made, and crease hard. Then repeat on the left-hand side.

29

STEP 4:
Turn the model over. Fold up the two bottom corners, and crease.

STEP 5:
Fold up the two flaps at the bottom of the model, and crease. You should now have a triangle.

STEP 6:
Fold the triangle in half. On the left-hand edge of the model, you will now have two pockets. On the lower right-hand side, you will have two points. This is one module of the ribbon.

STEP 7:
Repeat steps 2 to 6 to make 11 more modules, or triangles.

30

STEP 8:
To begin constructing the ribbon, slot the two points of one triangle into the two pockets of another triangle.

STEP 9:
Finally, when all the triangles are slotted together, slide the two points of triangle 12 into the pockets of triangle 1 to complete the circle.

STEP 10:
Cut a rough circle from your piece of cardboard. Write your St. Patrick's Day message on it. Next, glue the origami circle onto the cardboard. Cut two long strips of paper and glue them to the back. Tape on a safety pin and wear your origami ribbon with pride!

Glossary

Celtic
Related to or having to do with the religions, languages, and cultures of people and tribes who lived in parts of modern-day Europe.

commemorates
Remembers a person or event with a special ceremony or celebration.

legends
Stories handed down from long ago that are often based on some facts but cannot be proven to be true.

origami
The art of folding paper into decorative shapes or objects.

pagan
Relating to people from the past who followed religions that often had more than one god and were strongly connected to nature. Some pagans worshipped the sun.

symbols
Objects or pictures that stand for or represent another thing, such as an important event or person. For example, a cross may be a symbol of Christianity.

  # Index

C
Celtic crosses, 8
Celtic cross origami model, 8–9, 10–11
Christianity, 8

I
Ireland, 4, 8, 12, 28

J
Japan, 4

L
leprechaun origami model, 16–17, 18–19
leprechauns, 4, 16, 20, 24

O
origami (general), 4, 6–7

P
pagan religions, 8
pot of gold origami model, 20–21, 22–23

R
rainbow origami model, 24–25, 26–27
rainbows, 24
ribbon origami model, 28–29, 30–31

S
shamrock origami model, 12–13, 14–15
shamrocks, 4, 12
St. Patrick, 4, 8, 12
sun, the, 8

 # Websites

www.activityvillage.co.uk/st-patricks-day-crafts
www.kids-cooking-activities.com/St-Patricks-day-recipes.html
www.origami-resource-center.com/st-patricks-paper-crafts.html

Publisher's note to educators and parents: Our editors have carefully reviewed these websites to ensure that they are suitable for students. Many websites change frequently, however, and we cannot guarantee that a site's future contents will continue to meet our high standards of quality and educational value. Be advised that students should be closely supervised whenever they access the internet.